Thérèse Dufour
·
Marie-Claire Hamon
·
Delphine Renon
·
Translated by Dipa Chaudhuri

The ogress and the rainbow bird

Adapted from a traditional Indian tale

A tale along with postures for being stronger together

Om Books International

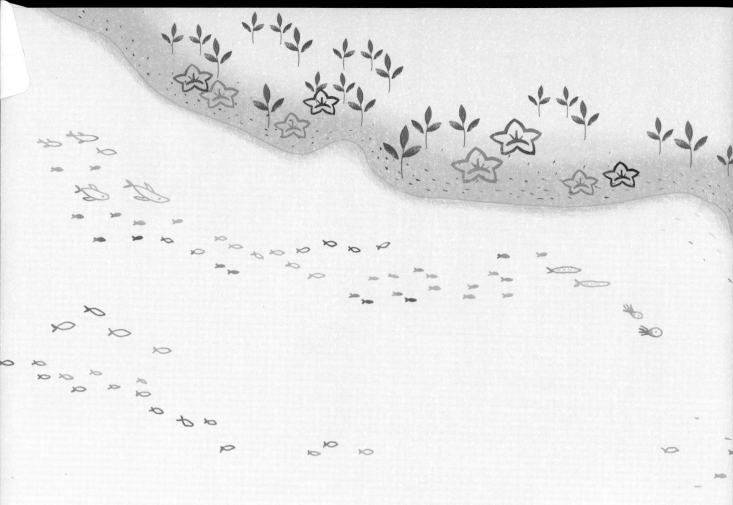

Listening to the lotus

To start with, get ready to listen to the story.

Benefits: While concentrating on his breathing, the child calms down and gathers his attention.

🕐 6 breaths

Sit cross-legged on a cushion.

If you wish, you could lean against a wall. Place your hands on your knees, with the palms turned towards the sky.

Close your eyes and breathe gently. You are ready to listen to the story.

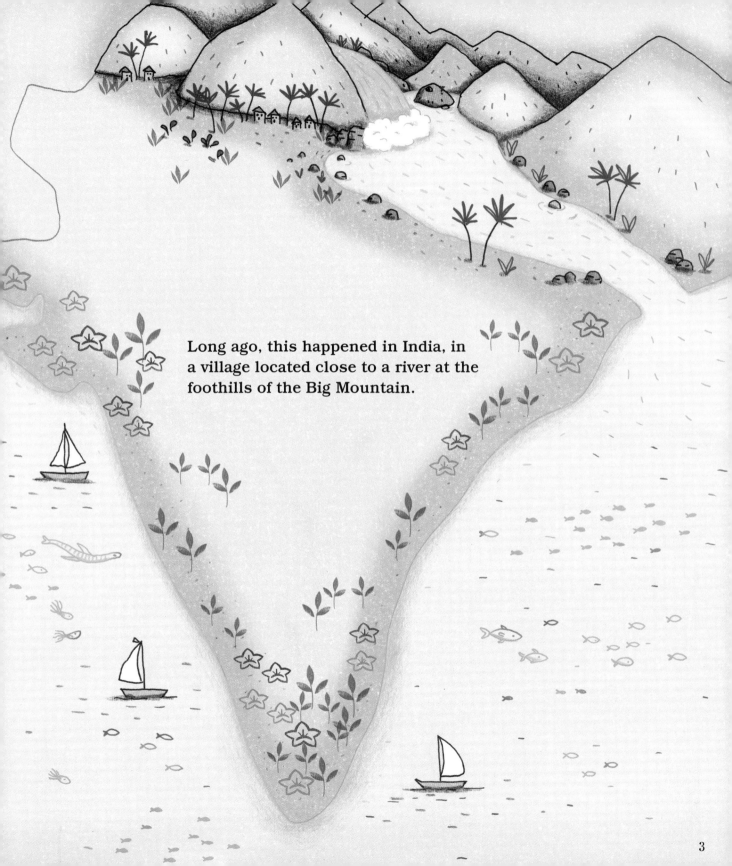

Long ago, this happened in India, in a village located close to a river at the foothills of the Big Mountain.

Behind a high waterfall, the cliffs form a reservoir, with an island on which, it is believed, lives an ogress.

4

"Children, do not stray beyond the waterfall for a bath. The ogress on the island shall gobble you up." That's what Kala and her little brother Shami hear each time they head out to the river.

Yet no one has ever seen the ogress...does she really exist?

On an unbearably hot day,
the children tell each other:
"How about a refreshing dip
in the river?"

6

Barely do they utter that, and off they go...
On the way, Kala holds her little brother's hand tight so he doesn't stumble on the sharp pebbles. And he is not scared of chasing away the snakes that so frighten his sister.

That's how they help each other...

The solidarity walk

Like Kala and Shami, learn to help each other.

Benefits: This walking together stimulates balance and coordination.

3 steps in front, 3 steps back

10 seconds

Stand facing the adult.

Place your feet on the adult's. Hold each other's hands, with your arms outstretched. Lean back while remaining straight.

The adult starts walking while lifting one foot. Your leg is folded while your foot is on the adult's. Continue walking together.

Sit down. Resting on your elbows, shake your legs in the air.

As they near the water, a song, melodious and pure as crystal, stops them in their tracks. It is sung by a bird that comes to perch on Shami's head.

It is so tiny that one can barely see it, but it has such extraordinary feathers: "Blue, yellow, orange, rouge…" murmurs Kala.

"Rainbow birds, that is what we are called," says the bird. "You too can sing as beautifully as me. All you need to do is bathe yourselves behind the waterfall. Follow me…"

The bird

Like the rainbow singer, spread your wings.

Benefits: This posture opens up the upper back and improves the coordination of the hands.

🕐 4 breaths

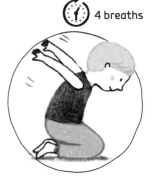

| Get down on your knees and sit on your heels. | Stretch your hands behind your back. The palms face each other, while the fingers are spread out. | Lean a bit in front and move your hands from the top to the bottom. You have wings and are ready to fly. | Straighten your back and place your hands on your thighs. Close your eyes and let out a deep sigh. |

Without a second thought, the children throw themselves into the water and dip their heads, laughing with happiness.

Alas! They did not see either the silver bridge rise, or the very tall and beautiful woman who is carrying them with an iron grip to the cold cave in the island. The ogress!

The silver bridge

Your body is as strong as the silver bridge.

Benefits: Through this posture, the child experiments with an inverted position in space which tones up the back and the stomach.

3 breaths   3 breaths

Lie down on your back. Fold your legs and keep them apart. Stretch your hands behind your head.

Make a bridge while pushing with your feet. Your buttocks and your back lift off the ground.

Lower your back gently.

Bring your knees to your stomach and embrace them with your hands.

"Finally children!" screams the ogress. "I have had enough of these tiny, tasteless birds. My dear meals, how lovely you both are. A little too thin though.

"You," says she to Kala, "you shall stay with me and cook for your brother. I would like him to be nice and plump. Let's put him aside…"

The ogress puts Kala down on the floor, opens a heavy wooden door and throws Shami into a dark room.

The children scream in a chorus: "If you separate us, we shall let ourselves die of hunger and thirst!"

Enraged, the ogress pushes Kala into the room that she locks twice, and cries, "We shall see that! A day and a night here shall be more than enough to make you change your mind."

They are together, but as prisoners! The children are overcome by a moment of despair.

Kala sobs: "Well, we have disobeyed... Who will come looking for us in such a place?"

Shami comforts her: "Don't cry, big sister. Together, we shall find a way out. Look at the stream of light deep inside the cave. There is surely an opening in the wall..."

Shami was not wrong: there is really a passage that leads outside. He puts his mouth on the tiny opening and makes a rolling sound in his throat like the people of his village have been doing for generations.

The rock amplifies the sound, and the wind carries this marvellous music outside.

A few seconds later, the rainbow bird enters the room through the tiny opening and settles down on the little boy's head.

It says: "Thank you Shami. Without you, I would never have found a way to enter this place. I had gone to the river looking for you so that you could rid us all from the ogress. She devours all of us and dresses herself up in our feathers.

Feathers

Your body becomes as light as the feathers of the bird.
Benefits: Through these lateral bends, the child gently makes his back flexible, with the help of the right breathing.

2 breaths

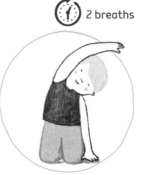
2 breaths

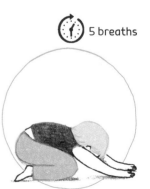
5 breaths

While seated on your knees, lift your hands towards the sky, holding them close to your ears.

Lower a hand to one side while bending to the same side. Breathe gently.

Straighten yourself, with both hands stretched towards the sky. Now do the same thing on the other side.

Bring your stomach close to your thighs, with your hands and head on the ground.

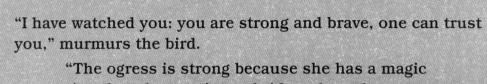

"I have watched you: you are strong and brave, one can trust you," murmurs the bird.

"The ogress is strong because she has a magic ring that changes into a bridge when she wants to cross the waters. Without the bridge, she would be a prisoner in her island; she would sink to the bottom of the river and drown!

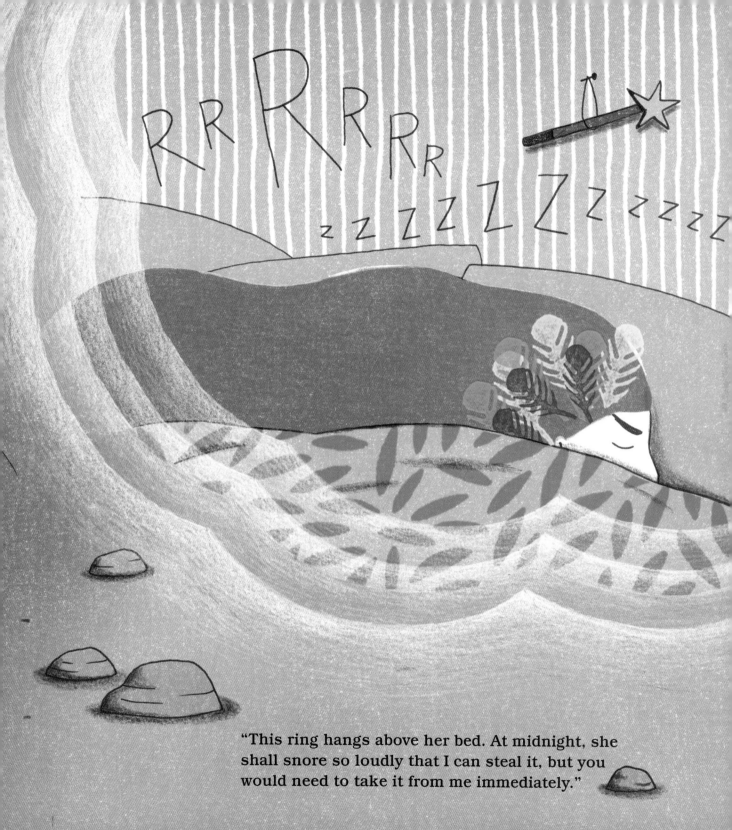

"This ring hangs above her bed. At midnight, she shall snore so loudly that I can steal it, but you would need to take it from me immediately."

"None can catch the ring faster than my sister," exclaims Shami.
"But without the key, how can we get out of this place? We are doomed," groans Kala.

"Don't worry, children, I am there…"

A rat who had sneaked in from under the prison door joined them. "One day, you had diverted a cobra that was on my path and wanted to eat up my little ones. Now, it is my turn to help you. While the ogress snores, I and my friends shall gnaw away at this door."

The rat

What if you were to help the rat free the children?

Benefits: Through this movement that stretches and opens up the neck and the back, the child learns to move quickly from mobilising energy to relaxing.

5 times

5 breaths

Get down on all fours.

Push your buttocks back towards your feet.

Now lift them up while keeping your head straight.

Roll to the side and curl up like a little rat asleep in its hole.

Listening to these words, the children become hopeful again. They feel themselves becoming as strong as a lion, as cunning as a monkey and as joyful as a chaffinch!

At the stroke of midnight,
the ogress snores...

Hundreds of rats run all over the
prison door. They gnaw and nibble,
and in no time, the door is reduced
to twigs on the ground. The children
are free.

Noiselessly, the tiny troupe approaches the ogress's bed.
With a swift movement of the beak, the bird unhooks the ring
and throws it at Kala who immediately catches it.

That's when the ogress suddenly stands up
on her bed like a spring. She reaches out for
the little girl. But the rats leap about! Over her
head, over her feet, in her bed…

The leaping ogress

Like the ogress who has woken up, you jump too!

Benefits: This posture helps experiment with briefly balancing on the hands without apprehension.

🕐 1 or 2 times

You are standing.

Place your hands in front of you on the ground while folding your knees.

While supporting yourself on your hands, lift your feet off the ground, jumping like a spring.

Sit down on your feet and let out a deep sigh.

The ogress screams and struggles in vain!

The children escape by the silver
bridge that takes them far away
from the cave, while the rats throw
the ogress in the river where she
disappears, never to be seen again.

Back in the village, the rat declares: "Prepare a big fire and burn this ring. And let the smoke that rises above your heads protect you all your life; only on one condition, stay united, for together, one is stronger!"

Smoke

Like the smoke, your hands grow lighter and lift themselves towards the sky.

Benefits: Thanks to this posture, to be done by two people, the child is mindful of the other through bodily contact. This way, he shares with the adult soft and soothing sensations.

Sit down cross-legged, back-to-back.

Lift your hands together towards the sky while inhaling.

Let your hands down gently and lightly by the sides, while exhaling. Repeat this a few times.

With your eyes closed, rock yourselves slowly together from left to right for as long as you wish.

Relaxation

The story is finished. Now you shall relax.
◎ **Choose a quiet place, with cushions and stuffed toys**
(or the blanket for instance).
◎ **Dim the lights.**
◎ **Make yourself comfortable and read these texts to the child.**
◎ **Speak slowly and softly.**

The preparation

"Repeat the following sentence many times: 'Your stomach expands and contracts like a small balloon.'

"Continue: 'Your feet, legs, hands, arms and head become heavy. Smile within as you close your eyes gently. We shall now travel on a magic carpet to a country far, far away.'"

The relaxation

"While you describe this journey, give your imagination free rein. You could also remember a place that you like or be inspired by the country described in the tale while returning to the Indian village on the banks of the river. The important thing is to remember the journey through the senses: touch, taste, smell. Also through the feeling of heat or freshness, sounds, colours, forms...

"For instance: You are close to an Indian village on the banks of a river. The sun is beating down on your skin. You soak your feet in the river. The current caresses and refreshes you. A tiny fish tickles your feet. The waterfall behind you makes beautiful music. From the village close by wafts the delicious smell of food. Now the sun goes down behind the hill. It is evening, and you return dancing on the tiny path that leads you back home."

Waking up

"Ask the child to move his fingers, his feet, to stretch himself, to yawn, and then to sit. Give him the chance to talk about what he has felt, without forcing him to do so."

To round off

"With hands joined over your heart, greet yourself while uttering the word '*Namasté*' from the Indian tradition."

Postures

This tale shows that when we help each other, everything becomes possible. Together, we are stronger and can accomplish great things. While doing the postures associated with the tale, the child identifies himself, thanks to his body, with the dangerous adventures that the two children live through, and especially with the way they help each other to emerge winners from these situations.

Listening to the lotus

p. 2

Namasté or greeting and *Padmasana* or the lotus

Benefits: Mobilising attention and calming down.

 6 breaths

Sit cross-legged on a cushion.

If you wish, you could lean against a wall. Place your hands on your knees with the palms turned towards the sky.

Close your eyes and breathe gently. You are ready to listen to the story.

The solidarity walk

p. 7

Walk together

Benefits: Balance and coordination.

3 steps in front, 3 steps back

10 seconds

Stand facing the adult.

Place your feet on the adult's. Hold each other's hands, with your arms outstretched. Lean back while remaining straight.

The adult starts walking while lifting one foot. Your leg is folded while your foot is on the adult's. Continue walking together.

Sit down. Resting on your elbows, shake your legs in the air.

The bird
p. 9
Uttanasana or the stork (variation)
Benefits: Coordination of the hands and opening up of the back.

Get down on your knees and sit on your heels.

Stretch your hands behind your back. The palms face each other while the fingers are spread out.

4 breaths

Lean a bit in front and move your hands from the top to the bottom. You have wings and are ready to fly.

Straighten your back and place your hands on your thighs. Close your eyes and let out a deep sigh.

The silver bridge
p. 11
Ardh Setu Bandhasana or the half-bridge
Benefits: Tones up the back and the stomach.

Lie down on your back. Fold your legs and keep them apart. Stretch your hands behind your head.

Make a bridge while pushing with your feet. Your buttocks and your back lift off the ground.

3 breaths

Lower your back gently.

3 breaths

Bring your knees to your stomach and embrace them with your hands.

Feathers
p. 17
Janu Konasana or angle
Benefit: Flexibility of the back.

While seated on your knees, lift your hands towards the sky, holding them close to your ears.

2 breaths

Lower a hand to one side while bending to the same side. Breathe gently.

2 breaths

Straighten yourself, with both hands stretched towards the sky. Now do the same thing on the other side.

5 breaths

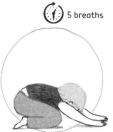

Bring your stomach close to your thighs, with your hands and head on the ground.

The rat
p. 21
Marjarasana or the cat
Benefits: Moving quickly from mobilising energy to relaxing.

Get down on all fours.

Push your buttocks back towards your feet.

🕐 5 times

Now lift them up while keeping your head straight.

🕐 5 breaths

Roll to the side and curl up like a little rat asleep in its hole.

The leaping ogress
p. 25
Bakasana or the crane
Benefit: Balancing on the hands without apprehension.

You are standing.

Place your hands in front of you on the ground while folding your knees.

🕐 1 or 2 times

While supporting yourself on your hands, lift your feet off the ground, jumping like a spring.

Sit down on your feet and let out a deep sigh.

Smoke
p. 28
Parvatasana or the hill
Benefit: Sharing of soft and soothing sensations.

Sit down cross-legged, back-to-back.

Lift your hands together towards the sky while inhaling.

Let your hands down gently and lightly by the sides, while exhaling. Repeat this a few times.

With your eyes closed, rock yourselves slowly together from left to right for as long as you wish.